The Legend of Mackinac Island

By Kathy-jo Wargin
Illustrations by Gijsbert van Frankenhuyzen

This book is dedicated to all children, whose determination and courage in life inspire us all.

Sleeping Bear Press
121 South Main
P.O. Box 20
Chelsea, MI 48118
www.sleepingbearpress.com

Printed and bound in Canada.

15 14 13 12 11 10 9 8 7 6 5 4 3

Wargin, Kathy-jo.
The legend of Mackinac Island / by Kathy-jo Wargin; illustrations by Gijsbert van Frankenhuyzen.
p. cm.
Summary: Retells the story of the great turtle Mackinauk that enlists the aid of other animals to help create the special place known as Mackinac Island.
ISBN 1-886947-12-0
1. Indians of North America—Michigan—Folklore. 2. Legends—Michigan.
3. Mackinac Island (Mich.: Island)—Folklore. [1. Mackinac Island (Mich.: Island)—Folklore.
2. Indians of North America—Michigan—Folklore. 3. Folklore—Michigan.] I. Title.
E78.M6W37 1999
[398.2' 09774;923]—dc21
98-56194 CIP

A legend

There are magical stories all around us, and they speak to us across the centuries. These are mythical stories created about characters so large, so strong, and so beautiful that neither time nor place can diminish their presence in our hearts. Such tales are told as a way to explain the most extraordinary figures of our imagination, as well as the most wonderful events of our natural world. These are the traditions of our time, stories that as both oral and written creations are lovingly passed from one generation to the next. And each time such a story is told it will continue to unfold and rejuvenate itself, inspiring the magic of legends.

There are many legends about the creation of Mackinac Island, each story as unique and individual as the storyteller. In our version, which is based upon the many versions that come from Native American history, the great turtle Makinauk (pronounced Mak-i-nahk) lends his back as a place for his treasured friends to rest upon. Just as there are many different versions of this creation legend, there are many different spellings of Makinauk; such as Makinak, or Makinaak. Today, the special place we know as Mackinac Island is always pronounced "Mak-i-naw" regardless of its spelling, and people of all ages have come to know the place of the great turtle's back as a haven of rest and relaxation.

Long, long ago, Earth was a quiet place covered entirely with water. There were no mountains or valleys, there were no forests or meadows.

There was nothing but one brilliant blue sea with a dark, murky bottom far, far below.

But life upon this giant world of water
was dazzling and bright. It was filled with
the rustling of waves, the splashing of ducks,
and the jumping of quick, silvery fish.

There were many animals here, and their
days were filled with laughter and friendship.

In the morning, loons carried soft downy chicks on their backs, keeping them warm and dry.

In the afternoon, otters played silly games upon the water, rolling their long bodies between the curve of the waves.

And while the other animals played, beavers bustled back and forth, slapping their flat and shiny tails upon the water. All around them, wee little muskrats tried to keep pace, their small, flat paws paddling eagerly against the waves.

In the midst of these fast
and playful animals
was one special creature
who was quiet and slow.
His name was Makinauk,
and he was the oldest, wisest
and largest painted turtle to
live in the great blue water.

Everyday, Makinauk floated upon the water in a calm and steady way. And as he floated, he would lift his large, wrinkled neck into the air and blink his deep, round eyes.

Makinauk carried the wisdom of centuries in his words, and always greeted his friends with a slow upward smile.

The animals were always delighted when
Makinauk floated by, because if they were
cold or tired, he would let them climb upon
his back to rest in the warm afternoon sun.

And if they were sad, he would sing sweet
and happy songs to cheer them.

And sometimes, when the air was still and the
moment was just right, all of the animals would
gather around Makinauk and listen carefully as
he told them wonderful stories about their great
world of water.

One day, Makinauk swam steadily toward the
other animals. His old weathered face appeared
quite serious, and in a low, broad voice he told
the animals how the Great Spirit of the Sky said
that now was the time to build a beautiful piece
of land for all of the animals to rest upon.

Makinauk then told the animals that one of
them must dive through the depths of the water
and bring up one handful of rich, wet soil, and
place it upon his back. This, said Makinauk,
would be the beginning of a brand new world.

The animals chattered with excitement, and the
wise old turtle raised his head and spoke clearly
to all of them—

> "I shall give to you, *a special home*
> *upon my weathered back*
> *where rivers run beneath the sun*
> *in red and gold and black.*
>
> To *rest upon the water blue,*
> *a land so new, a land so new."*

Naturally, Loon wanted to be the first to try, because she was the most loyal of all creatures, and always willing to prove her devotion.

She pulled her broad wings tightly to her back, stretched her long, graceful neck, and pointed herself toward the bottom of the world. Moments later she was up again, without a grain of soil in her bill. Disappointed, she hopped aboard Makinauk's back to dry her feathers in the sun.

Beaver, the most resourceful and hardest working of all animals, decided that he should be the next to try. He stiffened his back and twitched his nose, and with a loud slap of the tail, dove deep toward the bottom of the world.

Small waves rolled over the spot where Beaver disappeared. A little while later he rose to the surface holding nothing in his paws. He climbed on Makinauk's back and closed his eyes in sadness.

Then Otter decided it was her turn to try.
With a twist, a turn, and a flip of the tail,
she plunged into the depths far below.

Otter bobbed up to the surface several times,
each time diving deeper and deeper.
Eventually she reappeared, and with no soil
in her forefeet, she slipped onto the great
turtle's back and let out a long, soft sigh.

The animals rested quietly on Makinauk's back, feeling very sad. While they were sitting there, Muskrat came swimming by, and the weary animals told him about their struggle to grab a handful of soil from the bottom of the world.

Muskrat was eager to help his friends,
so he told Makinauk and the other animals
that he would dive to the dark and murky
bottom far below.

Loon, Beaver, and Otter laughed loudly
because Muskrat was the smallest and most
humble of creatures. His paws were tiny and
his back was weak. Surely he would fail.

But Makinauk did not laugh because he was kind and wise. And because he was a good friend to all animals, he smiled at Muskrat and nodded his head in a slow, gentle way, approving Muskrat's offer.

But the animals were still doubtful as they watched Muskrat take one long, deep breath, filling his round cheeks until they could hold no more. Then, much to their dismay, the little Muskrat closed his eyes and dove into the water.

Splish! Splash! Swish!

Little round bubbles popped up all around him as he made his way to the dim bottom far below.

Loon, Beaver, and Otter peered into the water, certain that Muskrat would never reach the bottom. They knew the journey was very long and dark, and they believed he would return quickly with no soil in his grasp.

They waited and they watched, but no Muskrat.

The animals waited some more, but no Muskrat. Time passed, and they began to worry. They felt sad that they had laughed so cruelly at their little friend.

Loon let out a long mournful cry.

No Muskrat.

Beaver folded his busy hands and lowered
his broad, dark face.

No Muskrat.

Otter stiffened her body
and sat straight and still
and was unusually
serious.

Still no Muskrat.

And as they waited, dusk began to fall, and the water shimmered in the fading sunlight. The animals searched every wave and swell, they listened to each splash and ripple, hoping to see Muskrat. But he did not reappear. The sky began to fill with the whisper of clouds, and all of the animals were hushed with sadness.

A giant tear rolled slowly out of the corner of Makinauk's eye.

Loon, Beaver, and Otter saw the tear slip down the great turtle's cheek, and began to weep softly in the moonlight for the loss of their friend and the hope of a new land.

But just then...

WHOOSH! Up popped Muskrat!

He flew to the top of the water with tremendous force, and his body was trembling with all of its might. His eyes were open wide and his cheeks were nearly blue, but wedged in the grasp of his small furry paws was the rich dark soil that was needed to make the beautiful new land.

Hooray! Hooray!

Makinauk nodded his large round head
in approval and said:

"I give to you, a special place
where sunshine crowns the land,
where flowers bloom like brilliant jewels,
everywhere you stand.

To float upon the water blue,
a home for you, a home for you."

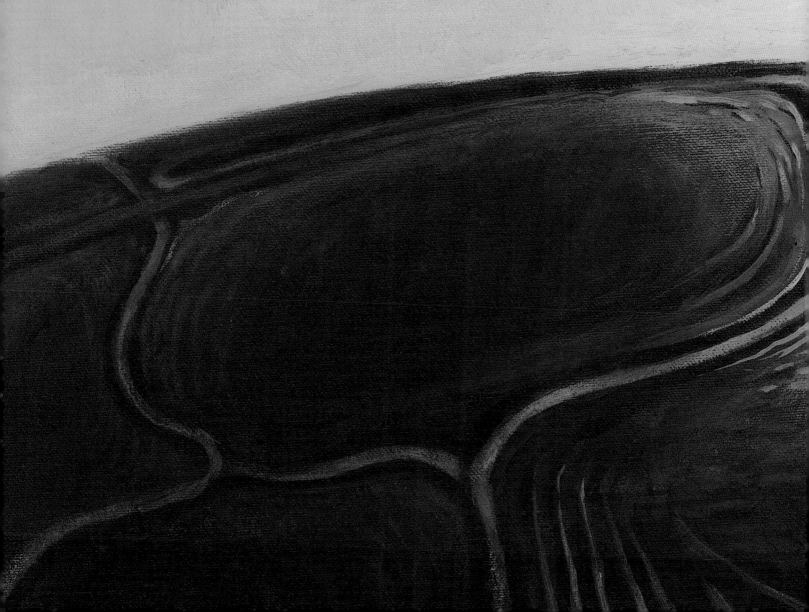

All of the animals watched in awe as
Muskrat quickly tossed the handful of soil
upon the great turtle's back.

Magically, the soil grew, and grew, and grew
all around them.

Rocks and trees and flowers appeared, and
sunlight poured down upon the bright new land
growing in the middle of the deep blue water.

And as the island blossomed, the low quiet voice
of Makinauk could be heard from all around:

"Time will now stand still, my friends
with an island rich and rare
And though we must part,
deep in your heart
my presence will always be there.

A special land that's edged in blue,
I leave this for you, I leave this for you."

The animals were happy to have such a lovely place to rest. It was a beautiful and splendid island, a glistening paradise of peace and friendship.

As the animals admired their new home, they noticed that Makinauk was gone. They began to miss the turtle very much, so in the spirit of his friendship, they talked about how kind and wise he was, and how he always shared his back as a place to rest.

As they talked, they realized that Makinauk was not really gone, because they saw his large round back in the shape of the island, and heard his deep, familiar voice roll through the rocks that line the shore. And with every wave and billow, they heard their old friend say:

I give to you this brilliant land
a place for peace and rest,
May forest paths and gentle waves
call you as their guest.

May sunshine drip like honey-gold
and sweetness fill the air
May diamonds fall upon the lake
and always glimmer there.

I leave you with an island home,
my sweet and treasured friends,
forever there upon my back
where splendor never ends.

And so to honor their wise old friend, they called the
beautiful new land **Makinauk Island**, the place of the
great turtle's back.

Gijsbert van Frankenhuyzen

After the enormous success of Gijsbert's first children's book, *The Legend of Sleeping Bear*, he has been very busy traveling statewide conducting programs. Painting is not only a career for Gijsbert, but also a hobby. That was the message his father taught him as a child and it is what Gijsbert tells all the children that he teaches. "If you can make your hobby your career, working will always be fun."

Gijsbert has been painting and illustrating since he was five years old and has produced hundreds of beautiful paintings. He feels, however, that except for his two daughters, Heather and Kelly, the best work he has ever created are the paintings for *The Legends*.

When he is not working on a book project, he still finds time to paint for prestigious art shows and exhibitions, bringing home many honors and awards. Gijsbert works from his studio on his 27-acre farm in Bath, Michigan, from where much of his painting inspiration comes.

Kathy-jo Wargin

Kathy-jo Wargin is also the author of Michigan's Official State Children's Book *The Legend of Sleeping Bear*, as well as *Michigan, The Spirit of the Land* which she collaborated on with her husband, photographer Ed Wargin.

With more than a decade of experience as a professional writer, she also conducts workshops, writing seminars, and educational programs for children and adults in schools and most recently, The Loft Literary Center in Minneapolis, Minnesota.

Kathy-jo's passion is to bring poetic detail to life, composing stories that can evoke deep emotions while opening doors to new places in the imagination. She and Ed reside in St. Paul, Minnesota with their son Jake.

MANITOU PAYMENT PT.

MANITO PAYMENT ID.

BREVORT CR.

BREVORT

BREVORT L.

MORAI

ROUN

PTE. AUX CHÊNES

POUPARD BAY

LAKE

MICHIGAN

ST. HELENA ID.

GRO
C

PT.

HAT ID.

ID.

WAUGOSHANCE ID

McGULF

WAUGOSHANCE PT.
(TEMPERANCE)

CEC
BA

CECI

STURGEON BAY

O NEALS

SUCKER CR.

STURGEON BAY

2

ILE AUX GALTES
(SKILAGALEE)

CROSS VILLAGE

WYCAMP
L.

BLISS

4

5

LARKS

LARKS L.

6

MIDDLE VILLAGE